THEY'RE FAMOUSE
THEY'RE FABU
AND THEY'
TO SAVE T
THEY'RE THE

HEROMICE

AND THESE ARE THEIR ADVENTURES!

Geronimo Stilton

ROBOT ATTACK

Scholastic Inc.

Copyright © 2013 by Edizioni Piemme S.p.A., Palazzo Mondadori, Via Mondadori 1, 20090 Segrate, Italy. International Rights © Atlantyca S.p.A. English translation © 2014 by Atlantyca S.p.A.

The publisher does not have any control over and does not assume any responsibility for author or third-party websites or their content.

GERONIMO STILTON names, characters, and related indicia are copyright, trademark, and exclusive license of Atlantyca S.p.A. All rights reserved. The moral right of the author has been asserted. Based on an original idea by Elisabetta Dami. www.geronimostilton.com

Published by Scholastic Inc., 557 Broadway, New York, NY 10012. SCHOLASTIC and associated logos are trademarks and/or registered trademarks of Scholastic Inc.

Stilton is the name of a famous English cheese. It is a registered trademark of the Stilton Cheese Makers' Association. For more information, go to www.stiltoncheese.com

No part of this publication may be reproduced, stored in a retrieval system, or transmitted in any form or by any means, electronic, mechanical, photocopying, recording, or otherwise, without written permission of the copyright holder. For information regarding permission, please contact: Atlantyca S.p.A., Via Leopardi 8, 20123 Milan, Italy; e-mail foreignrights@atlantyca.it, www.atlantyca.com.

ISBN 978-0-545-86796-2

Text by Geronimo Stilton
Original title *La carica dei robottini puzzoni*
Cover by Giuseppe Facciotto (pencils) and Daniele Verzini (color)
Illustrations by Luca Usai (pencils) and Daniele Verzini (color)
Graphics by Chiara Cebraro

Special thanks to Kathryn Cristaldi
Translated by Julia Heim
Interior design by Kevin Callahan / BNGO Books

12 11 10 9 8 7 6 5 4 3 2 1   15 16 17 18 19/0

Printed in the U.S.A.   40
First printing 2015

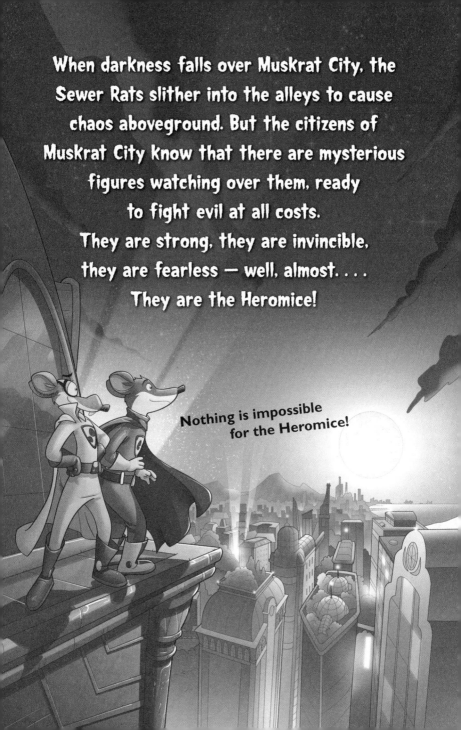

When darkness falls over Muskrat City, the
Sewer Rats slither into the alleys to cause
chaos aboveground. But the citizens of
Muskrat City know that there are mysterious
figures watching over them, ready
to fight evil at all costs.
They are strong, they are invincible,
they are fearless — well, almost. . . .
They are the Heromice!

Nothing is impossible
for the Heromice!

MEET THE HEROMICE!

GERONIMO SUPERSTILTON

The strongest hero in Muskrat City . . . but he still must learn how to control his powers!

SWIFTPAWS

Geronimo Superstilton's partner in crimefighting; he can transform his supersuit into anything.

LADY WONDERWHISKERS

A mysterious mouse with special powers; she always seems to be in the right place at the right time.

TESS TECHNOPAWS

A cook and scientist who assists the Heromice with every mission.

ELECTRON AND PROTON

Supersmart mouselets who help the Heromice; they create and operate sophisticated technological gadgets.

TONY SLUDGE

The undisputed leader of the Sewer Rats; known for being tough and mean.

AND THE SEWER RATS!

TERESA SLUDGE

Tony's wife; makes the important decisions for their family.

SLICKFUR

Sludge's right-hand mouse; the true (and only) brains behind the Sewer Rats.

ELENA SLUDGE

Tony and Teresa's teenage daughter; has a real weakness for rat metal music.

ONE, TWO, AND THREE

Bodyguards who act as Sludge's henchmice; they are big, buff, and brainless.

NIGHTTIME HERO CALLS!

It was a **FABUMOUSE** spring evening in New Mouse City. The sky was filled with stars and the moon was as round and *YELLOW* as a wheel of cheese.

Too bad I couldn't enjoy it. I was stuck at my office **DROWNING** in work. Piles and piles of papers covered my desk. It was the last day of the month and I had to review the budget of *The Rodent's Gazette*, the most famous newspaper in New Mouse City.

Rats!

Don't get me wrong, I love the paper. After all, I, *Geronimo Stilton*, am the publisher!

Still, I would much rather be writing than figuring out the boring budget. That night I had to keep PINCHING myself just to keep my eyes open.

Let's see here . . .

I was bending down under the desk to stick some papers in the **shredder** when suddenly the phone rang.

Rrrriiiiiinnnnnngggggg!

I sat up to answer it and **banged** my head on the desk lamp. **OUCH!**

The phone, meanwhile, continued to **ring**. Oh, couldn't whoever was calling sense a mouse in PAIN?

I picked up the receiver,

Emergency!

massaging the **bump** now forming on my head.

"Hello?" I squeaked.

"What took you so long, Stilton?!" a voice demanded.

It was my friend, **HERCULE POIRAT**, the mouse detective. I love Hercule, but lately, whenever he called I flew into panic mode. Somehow I had the feeling he wasn't calling to squeak about books.

"Well, I'm trying to work —" I began.

"**COSMIC CHEDDAR CHUNKS**!" he interrupted me. "Forget work, Stilton! It's an emergency! **MUSKRAT CITY** is in the dark. There's been a huge blackout! The rodents there can't even see their own paws in front of their snouts!"

"Can't they just wait for the lights to come back on?" I suggested.

Hercule snorted. "Super Swiss slices! Do you think I would call if it were that simple? This is a job for the **HEROMICE**! Have you forgotten already? We're famouse! We're fabumouse!"

Now, let me just say, that night I was *soooo* not feeling **famouse** or **FABUMOUSE**. But Hercule, or should I say, Swiftpaws, was in trouble. So I grabbed my **Superpen** and pushed the **SECRET** button under the clasp.

Immediately, I was surrounded by a superpowerful **green** ray that threw me **UP**, then **down**, then to the **RIGHT**, then to the **LEFT**. Holey cheese!

The Superpen that transforms Geronimo into . . . Superstilton!

All of the papers on my desk *flew* into the air. Then as quickly as a flash of lightning, I was thrown out the window (good thing it was open!).

SWOOOOSH!

Holey cheese!

Help!

A moment later I was FLYING through the star-filled sky. I didn't even have to ask where I was headed and when I would arrive. At that **supersonic** speed I would be in Muskrat City before I could even yell,

"Super Swiss slices!"

MUSKRAT CITY UNDER ATTACK!

I **BOUNCED** through space like a blind rat searching for cheese. Oh, why hadn't I read the instructions for steering hero costumes that *Swiftpaws* had given me? Even worse, I had no idea how to **STOP**!

The **GOOD** news is: I eventually stopped moving. The **bad** news is:

When I stopped moving, I began a fast **nosedive** downward. **RAT-MUNCHING RATTLESNAKES!** Where was I headed? Into a mountain? Into the ocean? Into a swamp filled with PIRANHAS? No, none of the above. I was going to crash into the rooftops of Muskrat City at full speed!

I zipped over buildings, **darted** down alleyways, and passed through clothes that were HUNG OUT to dry.

I was **tangled** up in: two pairs of pajamas,

Ooops!

a shirt, a dozen socks, and a GIANT pair of polka-dot underwear.

Finally, I landed on the ground!

THUMP!

"Seriously, Superstilton?! Does this seem like the time to bring your LAUNDRY with you?" I heard Swiftpaws snort.

Holey cheese! It was so *DARK* in the city I couldn't tell a rat from a cat! Where was Swiftpaws's voice coming from?

I freed myself from the damp clothes, struggling to sit up.

"Superstilton, we are in trouble!" exclaimed Commissioner **REX RATFORD**, the head of police in Muskrat City. "Little robots are looting the jewelry stores on Rat Avenue!"

"Umm . . . LiTTLE RoBoTS . . . did I get that right?" I mumbled.

"Yes," declared Ratford. "It seems that we are dealing with a gang of robots! They are taking advantage of the blackout to BURGLARIZE stores."

"What are we waiting for?" Swiftpaws asked. "Let's fly to the crime scene!"

"Sure," I squeaked. "Just give me a minute.

Aaaaaah!

I'm **TIRED**. I need to catch my breath. . . ."

But Swiftpaws interrupted me. **"Tired?"** he scoffed. "There's no time to be **tired**, Superstilton! Crime waits for no mouse!"

Then he grabbed me by my paw and exclaimed, **"Let's fly!"**

With a determined look, he stared at his supercape and yelled: **"Costume, activate Super-Slingshot Mode!"**

Let's fly!

14

Instantly, Swiftpaws transformed himself into a giant yellow slingshot. He pulled back and shot me into the air.

"HEROMICE TO THE RESCUE!"

he squeaked.

The Mega-Powerful Metal Head!

In less than a minute we arrived at Rat Avenue. When I landed I felt like I had been through a blender. My whiskers were twisted, my tail was *twisted*, my paws were twisted — even my eyelashes were **twisted**!

"Look over there!" Swiftpaws said to me.

For a mouse of many words, I suddenly found myself SQUEAKLESS.

In a corner of the street a police car had flipped over. A policemouse was being held up by a strange robot that looked like a gas pump. Another *ROBOT* was coming out of a jewelry store carrying two

OVERSTUFFED sacks. A few gems spilled from the sacks.

"What strange robots!" I exclaimed. "That one looks like a water boiler!"

"And that one looks like a bicycle!" Swiftpaws added. "Look! It even has *training wheels*!"

At that, the bicycle robot immediately tried to run over my hero partner!

Swiftpaws dodged *left*, then **right**. "Come on, Superstilton!" he shouted. "Let's show

Super Swiss slices!

these two **CLANKING** pieces of metal how we Heromice deal with trouble!"

"I-I'm coming," I mumbled, my whiskers **TREMBLING** with fright.

Oh, how do I get myself into these messes? *I'm not cut out to be a Heromouse!*

In fact, I'm a 'fraidy mouse. I'm afraid of everything — spiders, the dark, the ringtone on my cell phone . . .

I was so busy thinking about all the things that scared me, I didn't even notice the boiler robot had grabbed Swiftpaws.

Suddenly, a **RED** light lit up on the boiler and a stream of hot water gushed out.

Swiftpaws avoided it by a tail.

"Help!" he shouted. "Get it off me, Superstilton!"

I rushed at the **ROBOT**, but it pointed at

me, ready to hose me down with boiling water!

"Um, that's okay! I already took a bath today," I squeaked.

But when I reached out to push the boiler away, it was so hot that I *burned* my paw!

"FUMING FONDUE FOUNTAIN!"

I yelled.

At those words, my superpowers activated.

?!!

SUPERPOWER:
CHEESY FONDUE FOUNTAIN
ACTIVATED WITH THE CRY:
"FUMING FONDUE FOUNTAIN!"

A moment later, a *fountain* of cheesy fondue came streaming down right on the boiler, knocking it over.

"Cosmic cheddar chunks!" exclaimed Swiftpaws. "Your superpowers are out of this *galaxy*! What took you so long to use them?"

"Um, well, I was just waiting for the right moment," I mumbled.

Why hadn't I used my superpowers earlier? The truth was, I was so **FROZEN** with fear, I couldn't remember how to *activate* them! See, it's true — I'm not cut out to be a Heromouse!

I watched Swiftpaws deflate the tires of the bicycle robot. A second later, it was also down for the count.

But before we could declare victory, a blinding **FLASH** illuminated Rat Avenue.

"Give it up, Heromice!" a voice sneered. "Or should I say, **HOPELESSMICE**?! You didn't really think you could stop me, the mega-powerful **Metal Head** and my trusty robots, did you?"

A **STRANGE** rodent was standing before us. He had a mask on and a gadget on his head that seemed like a tube from a stove. **HOW BIZARRE!**

On his chest he had a glowing screen that lit up to indicate his mood.

ILLUMINATED SCREEN SHOWING METAL HEAD'S MOOD
CURRENT MOOD: EVIL!

Freezer Robot

Attack, little robots!

Lamp Robot

Next to him there was a fleet of little robots of all shapes and sizes.

"You don't scare us, you big, MOODY, metal monster!" Swiftpaws shouted. "You're no match for the Heromice!"

The criminal mastermind wrinkled his forehead and yelled, "ATTACK, LITTLE ROBOTS! The city will be ours!"

At that moment there was a strange noise. TICK-t-tICK-tICK-t-tICK-tICK . . .

My heart began to hammer. Was it a

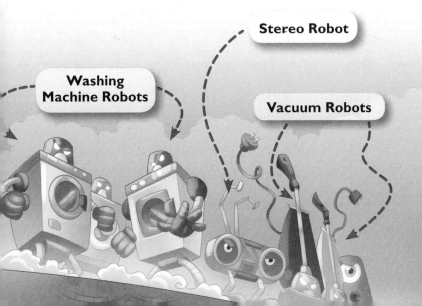

Stereo Robot

Washing Machine Robots

Vacuum Robots

ticking time bomb? Was it a crazed cuckoo clock robot?

"Get a grip, Superstilton!" Swiftpaws commanded.

That's when I realized the noise was coming from me! Fear was making my teeth **CHATTER** at a supersonic speed!

Before I could reply, Swiftpaws squeaked: *"Costume, activate Hammer Mode!"*

Immediately, Swiftpaws's costume transformed itself into a giant yellow hammer. Then Swiftpaws began chasing after all the robots.

They all fled except for one robot refrigerator with its doors **wide** open.

It stood in front of Swiftpaws.

"CAREFUL!" I yelled, but it was too late. My friend was trapped inside the refrigerator, which switched its temperature from "wintry cold" to "**Arctic frost**."

"I'll save you!" I yelled, yanking on the door until . . . **Super Swiss slices**!

The handle popped off and I **fell** backward into a pile of trash!

"Capture the fool with the **green** costume!" Metal Head instructed his robots.

But before **anyone** could move, another voice squeaked up.

"Give up, you **rusted** pile of junk!"

I turned in surprise. An athletic figure with a blue superhero costume and matching **sparkling** blue eyes appeared on top of a building. Her paws were set on her hips in a determined pose, and she wore a confident smile.

It was the amazingly brave **Lady Wonderwhiskers!**

HEROMICE IN ACTION!

My favorite Heromouse grabbed the robot **refrigerator** and opened it without effort. Swiftpaws rolled out, as pale as an icicle, his teeth chattering.

"Th-th-thanks Lady W-W-W-onderwh-wh-whiskers," he squeaked, staring into her eyes. "You're the b-b-b-best!"

I coughed. I admit it, I was feeling jealous. Can you tell I have a crush on Lady Wonderwhiskers? Yes, she is beautiful. But more importantly, she is smart, strong, and **BRAVE**!

I was about to thank her for her help when an awful stench hit me.

Good gravity! The smell was coming from

me! After that jump in the trash, I reeked.

Just then I got a **FABUMOUSE** idea. I approached the boiler robot, which was now out of order. I adjusted the thermostat and took a **HOT SHOWER**. Then I combed my **fur** with a little robot hair dryer defeated by Swiftpaws.

Finally, I was clean. I approached Lady Wonderwhiskers.

"Thank who . . . I mean, thank you Lady Whiskerwonders . . . I mean, Lady Wonderwhiskers," I squeaked.

HOW EMBARRASSING!

Luckily, my favorite Heromouse didn't seem to notice. "You're welcome," she said with a smile.

But a moment later her smile turned into a FROWN.

"Watch out!" she yelled.

Metal Head had unleashed all of his robot appliances. Sewing machines, electric stoves, televisions, and washing machines advanced toward us.

I was scared squeakless! Still, I didn't want Lady Wonderwhiskers to think I was a 'fraidy mouse.

"Heromice to the rescue!" I yelled confidently, even though my whiskers were trembling.

Police sirens screamed in the darkness.

"Retreat, robots!" I heard Metal Head command. "Take the jewelry and go!"

Right then a robot CAMERA ran toward us.

"Stand back!" ordered Swiftpaws.

But it was too late. A second later a giant FLASH lit up Rat Avenue, blinding us.

"Super Swiss slices!" cried Lady Wonderwhiskers. "I can't see a thing!"

"Let's follow them!" Swiftpaws suggested, but

Watch out...

Hey!

even he had lost his *bearings*.

Meanwhile, Commissioner Ratford had reached us and was bombarding us with questions about the little robot CRIMINALS.

"We really scared them off!" I said, hoping to impress the commissioner and, more importantly, the mysterious **Lady Wonderwhiskers**.

"Those little robots were terrorized when I hammered them!" Swiftpaws boasted.

"Oh yeah, well, what about when I covered them in cheesy *fondue*?" I added.

"That was nothing, Superstilton!" my partner countered. "I went up against ten of them on my own!"

I **ROLLED** my eyes. "**YOU** got yourself stuck in a refrigerator!" I retorted. "Lucky for you, *I* was there!"

"You fell in the **trash**!" Swiftpaws scoffed. "Isn't that right, Lady Wonderwhiskers?"

But the Heromouse had already left!

RATS! All we could do was say good-bye to Ratford and return to Heromice Headquarters.

Super ...
Yawns!

When we reached Heromice Headquarters, I passed out as soon as I **HIT** the bed. I dreamed I was living in a world made entirely of cheese. There were cheddar **sailboats**, mozzarella mountains, and Swiss-cheese sunsets. I was about to **NiBBLe** on a blue-cheese beach ball when someone yelled in my ear.

"WAKE UUUUUUP!"

I opened my eyes to find Swiftpaws standing over me.

"Wakey wakey, Superstilton!" he squeaked. "Crime never sleeps!"

I groaned. I was so **super tired** I could barely keep my eyes open. I am not cut out to be a Heromouse!

"Let's go, superpartner! **ELECTRON** and **Proton** are waiting for us for the operations meeting. And for breakfast," Swiftpaws added, **licking** his whiskers. "Tess Technopaws cooked a super-cheesy quiche!"

Lured by the super-cheesy quiche, I began climbing out of bed, but I got tangled up in the sheets. I **tumbled** to the floor, wrapped in the comforter.

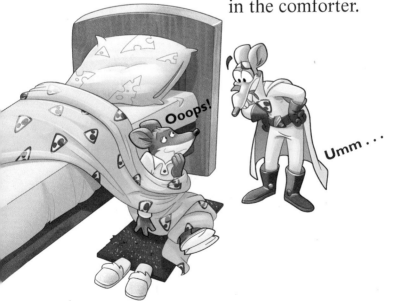

Ooops!

Umm . . .

"Does this seem like a good time for games, Superstilton?" my friend scolded me. "Now, come on!"

A few minutes later I was seated at the UANISHING table in the meeting room. The table was intentionally crafted for quick snacks. Too bad I was so tired I had to hold my head up with my paw! **Cheese and crackers!** If only I could use my superpowers to keep myself awake! Instead, I had to resort to pinching my own tail. OUCH!

Seated across from me, Swiftpaws wasn't just awake, he was super alert. He nibbled enthusiastically at the quiche **TESS TECHNOPAWS** had prepared.

The first thing about Tess is that she is a super cook. The second thing is that she is super brilliant!

"I'm wondering if the mysterious super criminal known as Metal Head might be an accomplice to **Tony Sludge**, Muskrat City's enemy number one," she suggested now as she sipped her tea.

"Maybe," said **ELECTRON**, Tess's niece and one of the Heromice's helpers. "But at the moment, no one knows where Tony is. Ever since he **ESCAPED** from prison, he's disappeared in the sewers of Rottington. No one has seen him since!"

"Very true," Swiftpaws said as he devoured the last piece of quiche. "By the way, have you discovered anything new about the robots?"

Proton, Electron's friend and an expert in computer science and supertechnological gadgets, typed something on the *KEYBOARD* of the computer. Immediately, black-and-

Hmm . . .

white images appeared on the screen.

"The footage taken by the video camera in Swiftpaws's costume leads us to believe that Metal Head doesn't use a REMOTE CONTROL to give the robots orders. His **little robots** probably respond to voice commands," Proton said.

"But it would be hard to give such precise vocal commands," Tess Technopaws mused thoughtfully.

Electron collected some papers from the printer. "My COMPUTER is creating a list of photos of all the Sewer Rats who are technological experts," she said.

Here's a list . . .

Tess and Swiftpaws

studied the LIST. Unfortunately, none of the rodents seemed to look like **Metal Head**.

SUPER, SWISS SLICES! This case was getting trickier by the minute! Even worse, I was still so tired I couldn't stop yawning. My eyes slipped closed until . . .

Boom!

I slid off my chair like MELTING cheese in a frying pan.

"Oops! Sorry," I muttered. "Yesterday was a tiring day, and then with the flight, the heat, **Metal Head**, and the attack of the little robot criminals . . . I mean, I don't even know how to work small appliances, let alone big ones."

Suddenly, Tess Technopaws **SLAPPED** her forehead. "That's it!" she squeaked.

"You are a **genius**, Superstilton!"

"Genius?" I mumbled. Too bad I had no idea what Tess was talking about!

You are a genius, Superstilton!

GUNTHER GADGETSNOUT!

Tess Technopaws put new data into the computer as Proton and ELECTRON looked at her in amazement.

After a while the image of a mild-mannered **Sewer Rat** appeared on the screen.

"Aha!" Tess announced. "It's Gunther Gadgetsnout!"

"Gunther Gadgetsnout?" I repeated. "Who's that?"

"Gunther runs an appliance factory in Rottington," she explained. "He would have the know-how to create ROBOTS like the ones that fought alongside Metal Head. Maybe he could even *be* **Metal Head**!"

Electron JUMPED to her paws. "I bet

File No. 546942
Gunther Gadgetsnout

Who: A mechanical engineer with a master's degree in robotics from Technotail University.

Where he lives: Rottington

Profession: He runs an appliance factory called Gunther's Gadgets.

you're right, Tess!" she squeaked.

Swiftpaws nodded excitedly. "I bet you a bunch of **BANANAS** he's the one!" he said. "What do you think, Superstilton?"

To tell the truth, I was still half asleep, but I didn't want my hero partner to get on my case so I said, "Um, yeah, I bet you a bunch of CHEESE RINDS it's him!"

Suddenly, my superpowers activated. A

SUPERPOWER:
A FLOOD OF CHEESE RINDS
ACTIVATED WITH THE CRY:
"A BUNCH OF
CHEESE RINDS!"

second later, the door **BURST** open and a bunch of stinky cheese rinds ROLLED into the room!

Holey Swiss sticks, my superpowers were strong! And the smell of cheese was even stronger!

Electron and Proton sat submerged in a pile of cheese, giggling. "Wow, your superpowers are SUPERTASTY, Superstilton!" they shouted.

"Um, yes, they are," I mumbled.

Wow!

Yum!

I didn't want to say anything, but sometimes my superpowers surprise even me!

While the rest of us **stuffed** our snouts with cheese rinds, Tess Technopaws studied the image of Gadgetsnout on her screen. "I don't know. Something doesn't seem right here. I know **Gunther Gadgetsnout**—we both took Robotics for Gifted Rodents at Technotail University. He wasn't like the other Sewer Rats. He wasn't into **money** or power. I can't imagine he would be interested in conquering Muskrat City," she said.

"Maybe he's changed. Maybe he became **friends** with Tony Sludge," suggested Swiftpaws. "But there's only one way to find out. We need to go back to **Rottington**!"

R-R-R-Rottington! Just the thought of going to that rotten Sewer Rats' den made my whiskers TREMBLE with fright! What can say? I'm not cut out to be a Heromouse!

"Are you okay, Superstilton?" Swiftpaws asked.

"Um, as a matter of fact, I am very COLD," I fibbed. After all, I didn't want anyone to know: I am a total scaredy-mouse! "You should go ahead without me. The sewer WATER is freezing. I might get sick," I squeaked.

"Don't worry. You'll be cozy and warm in the SUPERSUB," Tess insisted.

Brrr...

Super-Scared in the Supersub!

The supersub was Tess Technopaws's latest invention. It was a tiny **submarine**. Electron had created the motor, while Proton had designed the **sonar* system** that allowed it to avoid obstacles.

It was a flashy **yellow** color, and it was *floating* inside a secret pool that linked Heromice Headquarters to the sewers. It looked more like a floating piece of cheese than a submarine.

"Smoked ham and holey Swiss!" I protested. "Are you sure we need to take that thing? Can't we just walk? Walking is so underrated."

But Electron patted my back. "Relax,

---

*Sonar uses sound waves to detect obstacles.

Superstilton," she said encouragingly. "The SUPERSUB is easy to drive, and it will help you get around Rottington undetected. You'll be under the water's surface."

"Just hold your nose!" Proton advised. "The sewers are stinkier than blue cheese!"

What could I say? With shaking paws, I slipped inside the sub.

STINKY sewer water? Rotten, sneaky robots?

Oh, how did I get myself into these messes?

"If you don't mind, I'll drive, partner!" Swiftpaws insisted with a SUPERCONFIDENT tone. "You know how it is. I mean, I'm sure you'd be okay, but I'm probably much,

much better at **steering** this thing than you are. I don't want to end up in the wrong sewers!"

Soon we were seated in the cockpit of the **SUPERSUB**. Our watches **LIT UP** in superphone mode.

"Good luck!" Proton cheered.

He also explained that he would be monitoring our **movements** from the command center at Heromice Headquarters.

Finally, we plunged in and headed for a duct that led straight to the **SEWERS**.

Good luck!

At first everything seemed to go smoothly and I actually began to enjoy myself. Brightly **colored** fish *swam* by, and the water was crystal clear!

Then suddenly things changed. The water turned dark and ominous. Instantly my teeth began to chatter.

"Still cold?" Swiftpaws asked, fiddling with the temperature gauge.

A second later the submarine got so hot I was sweating like a furry *fountain*!

"Oops, I think I hit the super SAUNA button," Swiftpaws mumbled, twisting a few more dials.

A blast of FRIGID air filled the cabin.

"Hmmmm, this must be super air-conditioning," my hero partner went on.

SUPER SWISS SLICES! Would this nightmare ever end?

At that moment something slammed against the hull of the supersub.

Bonk!

"Did you feel that?" Swiftpaws asked me.

Bonk!

Bonk!

Bonk!

It was as if something was shoving the submarine!

I looked out of the porthole and my jaw hit the floor. Two enormouse eyes stared at me from outside. Two evil, glittering eyes attached to a gigantic, army-green crocodile body!

"What's out there?" Swiftpaws asked.

But I was so scared I could only babble, "The eyes . . . I mean, teeth . . . I mean, tail . . ."

Finally, I dragged my partner to the porthole. As soon as he looked out he turned as white as a ball of mozzarella. "COSMIC cheddar chunks! Since when are there crocodiles in the sewers?" he shrieked.

SINCE THE WORLD WENT CRAZY AND I BECAME A HEROMOUSE!

I wanted to scream, but I figured now wasn't a good time. Instead, I told myself not to panic.

Just then my watch LIT UP. I had almost forgotten that I could still communicate with Heromice Headquarters.

"Help!" I squeaked into the watch. "Save us! We're doomed!"

So much for not panicking.

Meanwhile, the $crocodile$ had chomped down on the back of the submarine and wasn't **letting go**!

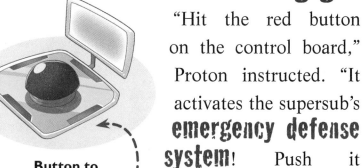

"Hit the red button on the control board," Proton instructed. "It activates the supersub's **emergency defense system**! Push it immediately!"

Button to push in case of a supersub attack

I hit the button and a $burst$ of air bubbles shot out of the supersub, $tickling$ the crocodile's belly until he finally let go and swam away.

I wish I could say we had time to **CELEBRATE** our victory, but we didn't. We had arrived at our destination:

Gunther Gadgetsnout's factory!

SOMETHING'S ROTTEN IN ROTTINGTON

The **SUPERSUB** approached the dock. Swiftpaws jumped out like a stealthy rat and hid behind some crates.

I tried to do the same, but a wave hit the supersub and . . . **PLUNK!**

Be brave, Superstilton!

I ended up in the stinky water! "Help!" I shouted. "I'm drowning! Good-bye, Swiftpaws!"

"Shhh!" Swiftpaws whispered. "Do you want them to find us?"

A moment later Swiftpaws **fished** me out of the water. I was so happy to be saved I tried to **HUG** him, but he pushed me away.

"Pee-yoo!" he squeaked. "You stink,

Umm . . . okay, I'm coming!

Superstilton! Let's hope we find a washing machine for that supersuit in Gadgetsnout's factory!"

Gadgetsnout's factory was super tall and **SUPER BIG**. One window happened to be open, but it was high up. Really high up!

My fur stood on end. Did I mention I'm afraid of heights?

But before I could protest, Swiftpaws grabbed me and took flight.

"Super Swiss slices!" I moaned, trying not to look down.

Inside the factory, Swiftpaws and I looked around. It was full of televisions, washing machines, and all sorts of other appliances.

"Look!" I said to Swiftpaws as I pointed to a **REFRIGERATOR** against the wall. The handle was missing, and it looked just like the refrigerator robot that had

attacked us the day before!

"Hmm . . . it looks like it's sitting on top of some kind of door," Swiftpaws observed.

Sure enough, there was a big IRON ring beneath the refrigerator.

"It's a *trapdoor*!" I cried.

We pulled with all our might but the trapdoor was stuck. It wouldn't BUDGE!

Cheese and crackers! I just knew there had to be something important hidden under that trapdoor.

"**OPEN UP! OPEN UP! OPEN UP**!" I yelled with exasperation.

And that's when the strangest thing happened. At my words, the heavy **METAL** door opened and hit me in the snout!

Ouch!

SMACK!

"Super Swiss slices! You're a genius, Superstilton! You guessed the *password*!" Swiftpaws congratulated me.

Password? Who knew?

Just then the trapdoor started talking in a robotic voice:

"SNIFF, SNIFF, SNIFF!

You smell like old socks!"

My partner chuckled. "Did you get that, Superstilton? Even the trapdoor can **SMELL** you!" he said.

I **BLUSHED**. After all, I am a mouse with excellent *hygiene*. But I couldn't think about it. We were on a mission. A mission to catch some robotic **CROOKS**!

We checked out the underground room. It was filled with mechanical parts and **ROBOTS** that needed repair. On one wall, there were **newspaper** clippings about the jewelry store robberies in Muskrat City. This was it! We had found Metal Head's HIDDEN lair!

"Let's hide upstairs and wait," I said. "We can catch Gadgetsnout — I mean, **Metal Head** — and finally go home!"

So we headed BACK UP to the factory. I was so happy we had solved the case! I couldn't wait to go home!

Unfortunately, in all my **excitement** I didn't notice a teeny tiny toaster on top of a shelf near the trapdoor. Without realizing it, I knocked it over and . . . HOLEY CHEESE! The toaster ended up on top of a juicer that tumbled onto a DVD player that crashed onto a microwave that landed on a shelf full of irons that fell onto a washing machine. . . .

In a **FLASH**, the appliances all tumbled down like a row of dominoes, making a tremendous noise. And when I say **tremendous**, I mean incredible. And when I say incredible, I mean unbelievable, and . . . well, you get the point. It was really, really, really loud!

"Oops!" I squeaked.

Right at that moment, the factory door opened. The lights turned on and a rodent with a deep voice **THUNDERED**, "Hey! What is that stench?"

Good gravity! We were in serious trouble now!

YOU'RE BUSTED, METAL HEAD!

Swiftpaws and I jumped on the mysterious intruder.

"You're busted, **Metal Head**!" I declared, snapping handcuffs on him.

But then I **LOOKED** at our prisoner and blinked. He was a chubby Sewer Rat with *ruffled* fur and kind eyes. He seemed **stunned**.

"Who are you?" he asked in surprise. "What are you doing?"

Uh-oh. I had a bad feeling.

"My name isn't **Metal Head**!" the mouse continued. "My name is Gunther Gadgetsnout, and —"

"That's enough, Metal Head," Swiftpaws

interrupted him. "We met you last night when you tried to **crush** us with your little robots!"

At that moment our watches began to **BUZZ**.

"Heromice, emergency!" ELECTRON'S voice sounded alarmed. "Muskrat City is in the dark again! There's been another attack

That's enough, Metal Head!

But I . . .

?!

by the little robot criminals!"

"But . . . but . . . that's not possible!" I yelled. "**Metal Head** is here with us in Rottington! We just captured —"

"There must be a mistake!" Proton interjected. "If you get over to the power station, you'll see that the robot attacks are still happening! You have to hurry!"

So we *jetted* out of the factory, paws flying, dragging a totally silent and confused-looking Gunther Gadgetsnout with us.

It wasn't until we settled into the SUPERSUB cockpit that Gunther finally spoke. "What is that terrible stench?!" he blurted out, holding his nose.

Rotten cheese rinds!

I was so embarrassed. That stench was

coming from my supersuit! And let me tell you, that stench wasn't just terrible — it was **deadly**!

Lady Wonderwhiskers in Danger!

The supersub emerged in Muskrat City in a flash. We raced through the dark city to the power station. And what we saw when we got there was really incredible.

The air was full of **SPARKS**, electric charges, and **BLUISH** flashes. Hundreds of criminal robots were *charging* their batteries with the city's power.

"Th-th-there are s-s-so many of them!" I stammered, fearing for my fur. "I think we're going to have to s-s-s-urrender!"

OH, I AM NOT CUT OUT TO BE A HEROMOUSE!

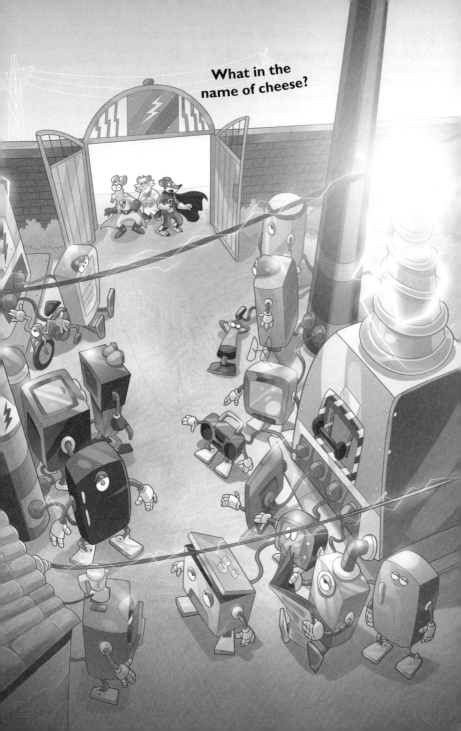

But then I saw a **horrifying** sight. It was the incredible, the mysterious, the brilliant Lady Wonderwhiskers! She was trapped inside an enormouse cage!

"We've got to free her, *Superstilton*!" Swiftpaws exclaimed with confidence.

I, on the other paw, was **trembling** like a super-scaredy-mouse.

Get a grip, Stilton, I told myself. *You're a Heromouse now.*

I imagined myself BREAKING through the gate and saving Lady Wonderwhiskers while everyone **cheered**. Then there would be a big party in my honor, with lots of cheese, and . . .

"Earth to Superstilton!" Swiftpaws's voice interrupted my thoughts.

I was so busy **DAYDREAMING**,

I had forgotten all about rescuing Lady Wonderwhiskers!

I shook my head and ran for the cage.

Lady Wonderwhiskers gave me a **BIG** smile. "Swiftpaws! Superstilton!" she cried. "You're here!"

Wanting to impress the **AMAZING** Heromouse, I threw myself bravely at the robot cage.

"Please be careful, Superstilton!" Lady Wonderwhiskers warned.

But it was too late.

Bzzzzzzttt!

The second my fur touched the metal bars, it began to smoke.

"Youch!" I cried.

"I wanted to tell you that it's *electrified*," Lady Wonderwhiskers said.

I tried to shrug it off even though my fur was so badly **singed** I made a mental note to make an appointment with Clip Rat the barber when I got home.

I was still thinking about Clip Rat when Swiftpaws sprang into action.

"Costume, activate Super

Hot~Mitts Mode!" he cried.

Immediately, my friend's paws began to swell up until they transformed into two enormouse **oven mitts**!

With one impressive move, Swiftpaws

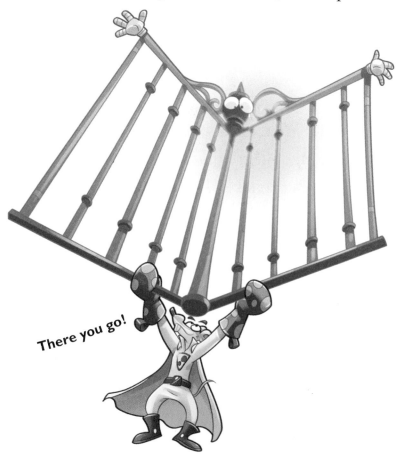

There you go!

lifted up the cage without getting a shock, and Lady Wonderwhiskers was free.

"Thanks, Swiftpaws!" the *charming* Heromouse squeaked gratefully. "That was fantastic!"

Swiftpaws smiled **TRIUMPHANTLY**, then shot me a look. He seemed to be saying, *Top that, Superstilton!*

Swiftpaws **tossed** the robot cage far away. Then he lifted a paw to his ear.

"Do you hear that, Superstilton?" he asked. "Get ready! They're *coming*!"

I had no idea what he was squeaking about.

"Wh-wh-who's c-c-coming?" I asked, my whiskers *trembling* with worry. Something told me it wasn't a bunch of old lady rodents welcoming us to the neighborhood with freshly baked **cheese** puffs.

I was right. Suddenly, an army of angry **ROBOTS** gathered before us, arms reaching, powerful parts clanging.

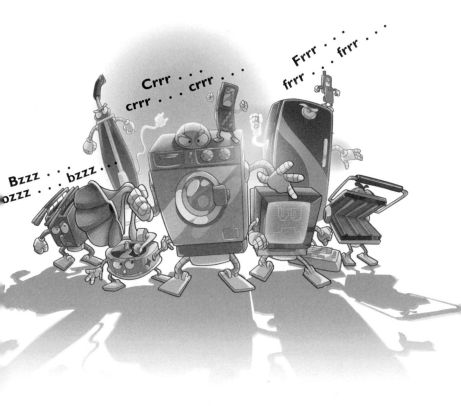

WHAT'S THAT STENCH?

The more I observed that **gang** of appliances, the more my whiskers shook. There was a sewing machine that looked ready to **EMBROIDER** our tails, a grill that could singe our whiskers right off our snouts, and two vacuums with **SUCTION POWER** that would leave us furless in a flash!

Lady Wonderwhiskers didn't seem worried, though. She calmly looked at the robots and sniffed the air. Then she turned toward me.

"What is that terrible stench?" she asked, wrinkling her nose in disgust.

I turned **RED** with embarrassment. "Well, earlier I, um, fell in the sewer and I um, couldn't shower, and . . ."

But before I could continue, the grill suddenly snuck up and grilled my tail.

SIZZLING SWISS BITS!

I let out an enormouse yelp and quickly spun around like a top, freeing myself from the grill's GRASP.

Oh, what a nightmare! My tail was roasted, my fur was burned, and I **stunk** so badly I could hardly stand being near myself!

Unfortunately, the robots weren't giving up. The vacuum cleaners *raced* toward us, along with a COLOR printer spewing ink.

"Melted mozzarella!" I shrieked in a panic. Immediately, my cheesy superpowers

Ouuuuch!

activated. What luck!

A great **GEYSER** of melted mozzarella **SHOT** out of the manholes, stopping the robots in their tracks.

A wave of hot cheese blasted the sewing machine and the microwaves! The vacuum

SUPERPOWER:
GREAT GEYSER OF MELTED MOZZARELLA ACTIVATED WITH THE CRY:
"MELTED MOZZARELLA!"

robots, however, began to VACUUM up the cheese, clearing the way for the other robots.

"Careful, Superstilton!" yelled Lady Wonderwhiskers.

But it was too late. A group of juicers were right on my tail!

Oh, what a way to go! I could just see the headlines now:

PUBLISHER PUREED BY PACK OF HIGH-SPEED JUICERS!

Clack!
Clack!! Clack!!!

Clack!
Clack!! Clack!!!

Save yourselves!

Luckily, Swiftpaws ran to my rescue. He turned into a **big** flyswatter and began to chase after the juicer robots!

It was then that a FIERCE washing machine appeared in front of me and Lady Wonderwhiskers.

"I'll handle this!" I squeaked, trying to appear confident. After all, it was just a washing machine. What harm could it really do?

"Stand **STRONG**, Superstilton!" Lady Wonderwhiskers encouraged me.

But when I turned to smile at her, the washing machine grabbed me, shoved me inside, closed the door, and began the spin cycle.

Vrrrrooommm!

I was **spinning** at full speed!

Once again, Swiftpaws and Lady

Wonderwhiskers came to my rescue. They
yanked open the door and I
slid out, half drowned.
On the bright side,
I was as fresh as
clean laundry.

"Oohh, now
you really smell
nice!" said Lady
Wonderwhiskers,
winking at me.

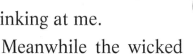

Meanwhile the wicked
Metal Head, the leader of the robots,
had returned to the scene of the crime.

"You got lucky, Heromice," he growled at
us. "But it won't last!"

Swiftpaws looked at **Metal Head**
and then at Gunther Gadgetsnout. He had
remained in a corner during the fighting,

where he had stayed completely **SILENT**.

"**SUPER SWISS SLICES!** So we were wrong!" Swiftpaws admitted. "Gunther Gadgetsnout isn't who we thought he was!"

"But then who is the *real* **Metal Head**?" Lady Wonderwhiskers wondered.

THE MEGA-ROBOT!

A sinister sneer appeared on Metal Head's snout.

"**HA, HA, HA!**" he snorted. "I'm just one big mystery! Good luck guessing, Hopelessmice!"

Right then Gunther Gadgetsnout took a step toward Metal Head. "Motormouse, is that you?" he whispered.

But Metal Head turned around and **disappeared**.

"Huh? Who's Motormouse?" Swiftpaws asked.

"What's Gadgetsnout SQUEAKING

Ha, ha, ha!

about?" Lady Wonderwhiskers added.

"I don't understand a **CHEESE CRUMB**," I mumbled.

Before we could figure things out, the roar of the appliances suddenly grew *louder*. As we watched in horror, two rows of vacuums latched on to each other. Then they **LINKED** themselves together with two large refrigerators, which grabbed on to the blenders, the microwaves, and the air conditioners.

"Cosmic cheddar chunks!" Swiftpaws shouted. "The robots are turning into one **GIANT** robot!"

By now my fur was standing on *end* and my whiskers were *whirling* with fear. Oh, I am **SO** not cut out to be a Heromouse!

Meanwhile the **mega-robot** was almost complete. The head was made up of televisions for **EYES** and enormouse speakers for ears. There were satellite dishes on top of its head, and its chest was five washing machines wide!

Super Swiss slices! What a terrifying sight!

At that moment the mega-robot began to take giant **clanking** steps toward us.

Clank!

Clank!

Clank!

The robot's arms and legs were made out of **MASSIVE**, industrial-sized refrigerators.

I tried not to look, but I couldn't help myself. The robot's horrifying, **FLASHING** eyes seemed to be staring right at me! My heart

H-h-helppp!

began to **hammer**. Stars swam before my eyes.

Luckily, before I could faint, Swiftpaws came to my rescue.

"Let's get out of here, hero partner!" he cried, pulling me by my **SUPERCAPE**.

A moment later the mega-robot's **GIANT** foot slammed to the ground right next to us, making a **huge** crack in the cement!

You Can Do It!

While Swiftpaws was busy saving me, Lady Wonderwhiskers had managed to jump up to the roof of a nearby building. She studied the giant robot up close, trying to figure out how to shut it down.

Then, without warning, the mega-robot captured her, CLUTCHING her in its enormouse refrigerator-hand!

Swiftpaws and I tried to free her, but the mega-robot *pushed* us away like we were two pesky gnats.

"Hurry, Heromice! Do something!" a voice cried out. "The other robots will tear you to bits!"

Who was squeaking? It was ELECTRON

Help, Heromice!

and **Proton**. They were communicating from Heromice Headquarters through our watches.

And holey cheese balls, they were right!

The little robots that hadn't joined the mega-robot rushed up to us. A DVD player **SHOt** a stream of disks at Swiftpaws, but he avoided them at the last minute by turning his costume into an enormouse DVD holder.

"Let's split up, Superstilton," my hero partner proposed. "I'll deal with these pieces of JUNK, and you rescue Lady Wonderwhiskers!"

Meanwhile, **Metal Head** had reappeared on the scene. He instructed an army of waffle makers to ATTACK Swiftpaws.

Good gravity! It looked like *I* was Lady Wonderwhiskers's only hope! But what could I do? I didn't even know how to fly straight, let alone rescue a Heromouse in trouble!

Still, as I watched Lady Wonderwhiskers struggle, a wave of anger came over me.

At that moment, Proton and Electron spoke to me through my watch phone. "Come on, Superstilton,"

Hang on!

Proton said encouragingly. "The future of **MUSKRAT CITY** is in your paws!"

"You can do it!" Electron added with confidence. "Save Lady Wonderwhiskers!"

I took a deep breath. They were right. I might not be the bravest Heromouse on the block, but I was still a Heromouse. I had to do something! Lady Wonderwhiskers and all of Muskrat City were depending on me.

"**Chunky cheese explosion!**" I squeaked as I launched myself at the mega-robot.

A moment later, my powers caused a very strange rain to fall.

It was a cheese rainstorm! **Chunky** slices of Swiss, **CUBED** bits of cheddar, and **balls** of mozzarella fell from the sky, **pelting** the mega-robot, slowing down its movements until it **creaked** to a stop.

"Come on, Superstilton!" Lady Wonderwhiskers yelled as she took advantage of the confusion to free herself from the robot's grip.

As quick as a rocket, I sped to her side and she jumped into my open paws. **HOLEY SWISS ROLLS**! I had saved the super amazing, smart, and **MYSTERIOUS** Lady Wonderwhiskers!

Still carrying Lady Wonderwhiskers, I flew around the **MEGA-ROBOT**. The giant robot spun around and tried to grab us. But the **FLYING** cheese chunks slowed the robot down.

The robot spun around and around

so many times that it eventually lost its balance and fell to the ground.

CRASSSHHH!

I couldn't believe it! I, GERONIMO STILTON . . . oops, I meant to say

You were super, Superstilton!

Thanks!

Superstilton . . . had **beaten** the tremendous mega-robot!

"You were **super**, Superstilton!" squeaked Lady Wonderwhiskers. Then she planted a super kiss on my whiskers. "You truly are a **HEROMOUSE**!"

"Well, um, thanks, Lady Wonderful, um, I mean, Whiskers, I mean Wonderwhiskers," I mumbled, turning as **red** as a ripe tomato.

Oh, why do I turn into such a **babbling** fool in front of my favorite Heromouse?

Still, there was no time to worry about it now. Just then, we heard a call for help from Swiftpaws. He was being threatened by a shredder robot with **SUPER-SHARP** teeth!

"**GIVE UP**, Heromice!" Metal Head sneered. Suddenly, the **STRANGEST** thing

happened. Gunther
Gadgetsnout turned and
yelled with all his
might, "No, *you* give up,
MOTORMOUSE!"

Metal Head stopped
the robot attack and

approached Gunther Gadgetsnout with **SLOW**, deliberate steps. When he reached Gadgetsnout, a **strange** expression came over his face and without saying anything, he opened his arms WIDE. **BLISTERING BLUE CHEESE!**

What was he doing?

What?!

TAKE THAT MASK OFF!

I was so worried that Metal Head was about to attack Gadgetsnout that my heart began **POUNDING** like a drum. Gadgetsnout was still in handcuffs. He couldn't protect himself. I couldn't let that happen!

So without thinking, I rushed after the **SEWER RAT** yelling, "Put those **Dirty** paws down!"

But just before I reached him, I tripped on my hero cape . . .

Oof!

Embarrassed, I stumbled to my paws.

"Stay calm, Gadgetsnout!" I squeaked. "I will protect you!"

"Thanks, Superstilton, but that won't be necessary," he replied, turning to Metal Head. "Isn't that right, Motormouse? Take that MASK off now. I know it's you."

We watched as Metal Head took off his MASK. Holey cheese, he was the *spitting* image of Gunther Gadgetsnout, but much younger. Who would have guessed?! Metal Head, or rather, Motormouse, was actually Gunther Gadgetsnout's SON!

"Well, that's a SUPER SHOCK!" squeaked Swiftpaws.

Gadgetsnout looked at his son sadly. "Oh, Motormouse, I was so worried about you when you left home. Why did you get involved with those Sewer Rats? You're

Sniff!

an **inventor**, not a **THUG**," he squeaked.

Motormouse lowered his gaze, ashamed. "Actually, I didn't really leave home, Dad. I built a secret *laboratory* in your factory."

Then Motormouse told everyone in great detail about how he had perfected the robots' **VOICE COMMANDS** and how Tony Sludge had been so impressed, he convinced the young mouse to help him steal from Muskrat City.

"That dirty, rotten rat criminal!" **Gadgetsnout** commented angrily. "How dare he **mess** with such a young, impressionable mind! I'm sorry this happened to you, son."

Motormouse sniffed. "No, Dad," he squeaked. "*I'm* the one who should be sorry. I thought you didn't think I was a good inventor. I was **MAD**, Dad, and I wanted to show you that I was capable of doing big things. But then things got **out of control** and I couldn't stop them. I was **afraid** Tony Sludge would turn against me."

After we took the handcuffs off Gadgetsnout, Motormouse embraced him.

Ah, there's nothing like a father-son reunion to make you feel all **warm** and **FUZZY** inside!

To make things right, Motormouse came up with a plan. He would give back all of the stolen jewelry and use the **ROBOTS** to fix all of the damage they had caused.

"And, um, then maybe you Heromice

could fix my factory in **Rottington**," Gadgetsnout suggested. "You really made a mess of the place."

Lady Wonderwhiskers looked at us curiously. "Really? The Heromice made a mess?" she asked. "How did that happen?"

Swiftpaws coughed. "Wasn't me," he said. "Maybe Superstilton can explain what happened."

Suddenly, it all came back to me. Knocking over the teeny, tiny toaster that HIT the juicer that **tumbled** into the DVD player that **crashed** into the microwave that *LANDED ON* the irons that **FELL ON** the washing machine that sent the rest of the appliances CRASHING to the ground!

Oh, how embarrassing!

ONE SWISS CHEESE POPSICLE

Armed with a broom, bucket, and mop, we spent the rest of the day cleaning things up at Gadgetsnout's factory. By the time we returned to Heromice Headquarters, we were beat! Cleaning is a lot harder than it looks! My back was **ACHING**, my paws were **throbbing**, and my stomach was **crying out** for food!

Lucky for us, Tess Technopaws had cooked up a whisker-licking-good four-cheese casserole. **YUM!**

As I dug into my **first** slice of the cheesy pie (well, okay, it was my *THIRD* slice, but who's counting?), Electron and Proton filled us in on the latest news.

It turned out that Motormouse posing as **Metal Head** had hidden all of the stolen jewels in an enormous freezer. When **Tony Sludge** arrived to get the jewels, Motormouse had already returned them. The only thing left in the freezer was one old *SWISS CHEESE POPSICLE!*

We all burst out laughing picturing the rotten Sewer Rat's shocked face when he discovered the lone cheese Popsicle.

Soon it was time for me to return to New Mouse City. A part of me was thrilled to be going home, but another part of me was going to miss my friends at Heromice Headquarters.

"Come back soon, Superstilton!" said Electron and Proton as they **SQUEEZED** me in a hug.

"I will," I agreed.

Finally, I hugged Tess Technopaws and said good-bye to Swiftpaws.

"See you back home," said my hero partner. "And don't forget to always keep that **SUPERPEN** with you and practice using your superpowers. Oh, and you might want to start *hitting* the gym. Try the **treadmill**, the weight room, or take a class. Something like Strength Training for the Slower Rodent or **TONE YOUR COUCH POTATO TAIL** would do you good."

I quickly turned to leave. What

Come back soon!

Great job!

can I say? I'm not a GYM RAT!

As I adjusted my cape, I gave my **supercostume** precise instructions: "Go slowly!"

Too bad my costume had ideas of its own. Before I knew it, I was SHOOTING into the sky like a furry rocket. Terrified, I yelled, **"NEXT TIME I'M TAKING THE TRAAAAAIN!"**

Helpppp!

THE RETURN TO NEW MOUSE CITY

As I flew home, I crossed through the dining room of a family of rodents. How **embarrassing**!

Then I broke through a giant billboard,

flew through a barn, and almost got **TANGLED** in some electrical power lines. **How shocking!**

I had asked my SUPERCOSTUME to take me home, but for some reason I found myself **HURTLING** through the open window of my office at *The Rodent's Gazette*. I landed on the top of a tall cabinet, after having circled the room a few times.

The noise attracted the attention of my sister, Thea, who was in the office next door. She BURST into the room.

"Um, Gerrykins, what are you doing up there?" Thea asked with a mixture of exasperation and concern.

Luckily, I was back in my *green* suit and my supercostume had vanished.

"Oh, er, I was just . . . **dusting**. Yes, dusting," I responded, trying to act normal.

Thea **rolled** her eyes.

"What is up with you lately, Gerry Berry?" she squeaked. "Yesterday you didn't come to work, and today I find you sitting on **TOP** of the cabinet!"

"Well, yesterday I caught a cold — *cough, cough* — so I stayed home. And today I'm just cleaning . . ." My voice **trailed** off as I looked down. How would I get down without my superpowers?

Super Swiss slices! I was so **HIGH UP**!

Oh, no thanks!

"Um, Thea, can you get a LADDER?" I asked sheepishly.

Thea came back to my office with a ladder. "Need a paw?" she asked.

Need a paw?

"Uh, no thanks," I replied. "After everything I tackled today, getting down will be nothing!"

Thea squinted up at me. "And what have you TACKLED today?" she asked, PERPLEXED.

"Um, well, the m-m-mess, the papers, the office," I stammered.

In fact, my office was a real DISASTER area!

Thea looked around and shook her head.

"Well, I'd say you still have a lot to do!" she said. "This place is still a mess!"

I climbed down the ladder and got right to work straightening up. It was a **supermess**! And it would take **HARD** work to clean it up. But if there was one thing I had learned that week, it was this: Nothing is impossible for the **HEROMICE**!

 **Don't miss any of my other fabumouse adventures!**

#1 Lost Treasure of the Emerald Eye

#2 The Curse of the Cheese Pyramid

#3 Cat and Mouse in a Haunted House

#4 I'm Too Fond of My Fur!

#5 Four Mice Deep in the Jungle

#6 Paws Off, Cheddarface!

#7 Red Pizzas for a Blue Count

#8 Attack of the Bandit Cats

#9 A Fabumouse Vacation for Geronimo

#10 All Because of a Cup of Coffee

#11 It's Halloween, You 'Fraidy Mouse!

#12 Merry Christmas, Geronimo!

#13 The Phantom of the Subway

#14 The Temple of the Ruby of Fire

#15 The Mona Mousa Code

#16 A Cheese-Colored Camper

#17 Watch Your Whiskers, Stilton!

#18 Shipwreck on the Pirate Islands

#19 My Name Is Stilton, Geronimo Stilton

#20 Surf's Up, Geronimo!

#21 The Wild, Wild West

#22 The Secret of Cacklefur Castle

A Christmas Tale

#23 Valentine's Day Disaster

#24 Field Trip to Niagara Falls

#25 The Search for Sunken Treasure

#26 The Mummy with No Name

#27 The Christmas Toy Factory

#28 Wedding Crasher

#29 Down and Out Down Under

#30 The Mouse Island Marathon

#31 The Mysterious Cheese Thief

Christmas Catastrophe

#32 Valley of the Giant Skeletons

#33 Geronimo and the Gold Medal Mystery

#34 Geronimo Stilton, Secret Agent

#35 A Very Merry Christmas

#36 Geronimo's Valentine

#37 The Race Across America

#38 A Fabumouse School Adventure

#39 Singing Sensation

#40 The Karate Mouse

#41 Mighty Mount Kilimanjaro

#42 The Peculiar Pumpkin Thief

#43 I'm Not a Supermouse!

#44 The Giant
Diamond Robbery

#45 Save the White
Whale!

#46 The Haunted
Castle

#47 Run for the Hills,
Geronimo!

#48 The Mystery in
Venice

#49 The Way of
the Samurai

#50 This Hotel Is
Haunted!

#51 The Enormouse
Pearl Heist

#52 Mouse in Space!

#53 Rumble in
the Jungle

#54 Get into Gear,
Stilton!

#55 The Golden
Statue Plot

#56 Flight of the
Red Bandit

Special
Edition!

The Hunt for the
Golden Book

#57 The Stinky
Cheese Vacation

#58 The Super
Chef Contest

#59 Welcome to
Moldy Manor

Special
Edition!

The Hunt for the
Curious Cheese

#60 The Treasure of
Easter Island

#61 Mouse House
Hunter

Don't miss
my journeys
through time!

Be sure to read all of our magical special edition adventures!

THE KINGDOM OF FANTASY

THE QUEST FOR PARADISE:
THE RETURN TO THE KINGDOM OF FANTASY

THE AMAZING VOYAGE:
THE THIRD ADVENTURE IN THE KINGDOM OF FANTASY

THE DRAGON PROPHECY:
THE FOURTH ADVENTURE IN THE KINGDOM OF FANTASY

THE VOLCANO OF FIRE:
THE FIFTH ADVENTURE IN THE KINGDOM OF FANTASY

THE SEARCH FOR TREASURE:
THE SIXTH ADVENTURE IN THE KINGDOM OF FANTASY

THE ENCHANTED CHARMS:
THE SEVENTH ADVENTURE IN THE KINGDOM OF FANTASY

THE PHOENIX OF DESTINY:
AN EPIC KINGDOM OF FANTASY ADVENTURE

THEA STILTON: THE JOURNEY TO ATLANTIS

THEA STILTON: THE SECRET OF THE FAIRIES

THEA STILTON: THE SECRET OF THE SNOW

THEA STILTON: THE CLOUD CASTLE